THE CROSS RABBIT

NICK BUTTERWORTH

TED SMART

It was a bright, cold winter's day.
Snow had fallen in the night and
now everything in the park had been
turned into a guessing game.

"It looks wonderful," said Percy the
park keeper, "but it makes a lot of work."

Standing next to Percy was a rather
old and cross looking rabbit.

"Well, quite so," said the rabbit.
"But now, what about these mice?
They're making a dreadful nuisance
of themselves."

Percy found it hard not to laugh
when he saw what was making
the rabbit so cross.

The mice were having great fun.

Percy began to chuckle, but quickly
turned the chuckle into a cough. After
all, this was no fun for an old rabbit
who only wanted to curl up and sleep
through the cold weather.

"Now come along, you mice," said Percy. "You must go and play somewhere else. And," he added, "try to stay out of mischief."

The mice looked very disappointed. Slowly they walked away, dragging their toboggans behind them.

The old rabbit said thank you to Percy and then disappeared into his burrow.

Percy got on with clearing the snow. It was hot work even in the cold weather. First he took off his cap. Then his scarf. And then, even his gloves.

Percy worked hard all morning.
He mopped his brow again and
looked at his work.

"Very good," he said to himself.
"I think I deserve a spot of lunch."

Percy reached for his bag and pulled out a flask.

"That's funny," he said. "I'm sure I put the cup on the top this morning."

"I know, I'll have my yogurt first and drink from the empty carton."

Percy took out a strawberry yogurt and began to rummage through his bag. "That's odd," he said. "No spoon. Hmm."

It was a strange lunch. A lid was missing from a small box of dates and the bottom half of one of Percy's cheese rolls had disappeared. And Percy was sure he had packed an orange but there was no sign of it now. It was all very puzzling.

It felt colder to Percy as he went back to
work. He reached for his scarf and his
cap, but now they had disappeared too!

" This is most peculiar," said Percy.
Then, as he gazed around looking
for his cap and scarf, Percy was amazed to
see his gloves walking off by themselves!

"I must be dreaming," said Percy.
"I'd like to be dreaming," said a cross
voice. It was the old rabbit again.
"Those mice are making a terrible noise.
Would you speak to them please?" And with
that the rabbit stumped off.
Percy followed.

"Look!" said the rabbit.
Percy looked. The mice had been
very busy indeed! And they were having
a marvellous time.

"Hello Percy!" they called. But suddenly
they looked worried. "You're not going to
tell us to stop, are you?"

Percy glanced at the old rabbit.

"Well. . .no," he said to the mice.
"We just wondered if you could
have a marvellous time a little
more quietly?"

The mice cheered.

"We'll try!" they squeaked loudly.

"Come on," said Percy to the rabbit. "I think I've got some cotton wool in my bag. A little in each ear should do the trick."

Nick Butterworth

Nick Butterworth was born in North London in 1946 and grew up in a sweet-shop in Essex. He now lives in Suffolk with his wife Annette and their two children, Ben and Amanda.

The inspiration for the Percy's Park books came from Nick's many walks through the local park with the family dog, Jake. *One Snowy Night,* the first story about Percy the park keeper and his animal friends, was published in 1989 and was an instant success. Now stories about Percy and his friends are firm favourites with children everywhere.